What others are saying about this book:

Your book really works. I decided to try using Images, Pictures and Thoughts on my two dogs instead of just words and it works.... I was truly amazed...

—Christina

I was able to bring closure on two dogs that had to be put down when I was a young girl. What a wonderful book to teach children that it is part of life when a beloved pet has to leave the earth. To learn that they are more than ok. They are healthy and happy once again.

—doni

This is definitely a book for all ages, from child to adults. There is something for everyone. I laughed and cried, then laughed and cried again. When I got to the end, I just felt so good, happy and peaceful.

—Dorothy

Samantha's love story is just that. It's about the love a dog has for their owner and the love that the owner has for their dog. Samantha's story tugs at the heartstrings. Through Samantha's instructions, you to can start to understand how to communicate with your pet and how your pet managed to find you. The story goes through her whole life, even up to and past her death. You can learn to communicate with your pet and enjoy the special bond you'll have after learning to understand your pet. This is a warm, poignant story that is well written and enjoyable. See through Samantha's eyes and enjoy!

—Barbara

The book shows when learning how to relate to animals, it can also help in relating to humans. It has helped me become more aware and sensitive to the needs of others.

—Susan V.

Samantha's Love Story

Samantha's Love Story

✦

A Guide on Psychic Communication with Animals

By: Patricia Daniels

iUniverse, Inc.
New York Lincoln Shanghai

Samantha's Love Story
A Guide on Psychic Communication with Animals

iUniverse, Inc.

For information address:
iUniverse, Inc.
2021 Pine Lake Road, Suite 100
Lincoln, NE 68512
www.iuniverse.com

First Printing: 2004
Photographs by: Marie Fuller

ISBN: 0-595-31065-6

Printed in the United States of America

Contents

Introduction

During the span of time that I've known Patricia Daniels, she has touched my heart like no other human being. She is a loving, caring, considerate woman, who is devoted to Samantha and Sati.

Patricia is a passionate woman, driven by her love for animals. She is a compassionate human, concerned about the welfare of all animals species; concerned for more than just the ownership of all her furry friends throughout her lifetime.

This is a story written through the eyes of her beloved Samantha. A story filled with fun, love, mischief and most of all, the bond between a human and an animal.

With love, I introduce you to Pat and Samantha!!
Princess Lavada Starr Mawuli
Celebrity Publicist

What dogs?
These are my children.
Little people with fur
who make my heart open a little wider.
Oprah Winfrey

Acknowledgements

In Memory of Samantha
My furry, spiritual guide
who taught me true communication.

I thank God for the creation of Samantha.

Gwen, for finding and rescuing this little girl
on the first 30 degree night in Gainesville.

My son, **Eric,** who continued the process of bringing this six
week bundle of energy into my life.

Trish Rozzell, for planting the seed and direction
this book would take.

My granddaughter, **Jessi,** when reading a couple of pages
of the book's first draft said, "Oh Gramma,
this is so awesome!" inspiring me further.

My friends, **Christina De Cos. Sabrina Scott** and **Michael Hickland,** my constant sources of encouraging, gentle
prodding that kept me moving forward with the book.

Sue Ann Valdez, a tender empathetic soul
and dear friend, who was a source of comfort
to both Samantha and myself during her final days.

Bruce D. Horchak, D.C. and **Marty Horchak,**
for keeping my body, mind and spirit together
during Samantha's illness and her passing on.

Dr. Betsy Coville, who through her knowledge of alternative
medicine gave Samantha the gift
of an additional three years of quality life.

Vet Care Animal Hospital for understanding that the time
had come to administer conventional medicine to make
Samantha's last days comfortable.

Florida Veterinary Specialists,
Tamara Berlin, D.V.M. and her staff,
performing their professional, swift, caring manner assisting
Samantha in her last moments.

doni Rae, my earth angel,
who walked with me through the book's progression.

**No one appreciates the very spiritual genius
of your conversation as the dog does.
Christopher Morley**

Everybody is born so they can learn
how to live a good life,
like loving everybody and being nice right?
Well, animals already know how to do that,
so they don't have to stay as long.

From the book "Chicken Soup for the Pet Lover's Soul
and Animals Passing on..
Words of wisdom shared by a 4yo child.

A newly discovered chapter in the Book of Genesis has provided the answer to **"Where do pets come from?"**

Adam and Eve said "*Lord when we were in the garden, you walked with us every day. Now we do not see you anymore. We are lonesome here, and it is difficult for us to remember how much you love us.*"

And God said "*No problem! I will create a companion for you that will be with you forever and who will be a reflection of my love for you, so that you will love me even when you cannot see me. Regardless of how selfish or childish or unlovable you may be, this new companion will accept you as you are and will love you as I do, in spite of yourselves.*"

And God created a new animal to be a companion for Adam and Eve. And it was a good animal. And God was pleased. And the new animal was pleased to be with Adam and Eve and he wagged his tail.

And Adam said, "*Lord, I have already named all the animals in the Kingdom and I cannot think of a name for this new animal.*"

And God said, "*No problem. Because I have created this new animal to be a reflection of my love for you, his name will be a reflection of my own name, and you will call him* ***DOG.***"

A righteous man has regard for the life of his beast.
Proverbs 12:10

Foreword

Like all books written in this manner, some thoughts and ideas may challenge your belief system. It is all right whether or not you choose to believe what is written here. My mission is simply to help open your eyes to look into ours, to appreciate our intelligence even though a different species from you.

This is a love story, a love between a human species and animal species. It is a story of two souls connecting, helping each other evolve to a higher plane of understanding and communication. It is a story seen through the eyes of a beloved spirit in the form of a canine species and written through the heart core of a tender, loving human species. It is written with humor, instruction and love.

Learning to communicate with animals is vital. It teaches you to open up your hearts. It teaches you to let go of fear, to become sensitive. It will force you to examine your life. Your problems will be taken on in some form in your animal if you aren't careful. When there is a problem, look at yourself. See where it is coming from. Your animal is your mirror, reflecting what needs fixing.

This is a time of danger of possible extinction of all species. Humans included. You need to look into the hearts and minds of all living creatures. This story will hopefully help you look at your animal friend that you chose to be a guardian to. You are spirit. All spirit is one. As you learn to accept that and treat all creatures with love and respect, therein stands the chance of saving the planet Earth.

We all are the energy of life, ongoing, ongoing….

1

From One Heart to Another

How It All Began

Living is life and being aware of life.
Unknown

Gentle hands. Gentle cooing noises. Gentle massage. Cleaning of my eyes with a damp washcloth. Nose gently massaged with a soothing Elk Antler cream. Drops of Gatorade to moisten my throat and elevate my electrolytes and thyroid medication. These are the ministrations that I wake up to each morning.

Close body warmth, gentle rocking, warm breath on my body when I am having one of my shaking spells. Fingers helping my fumbling mouth accept warm food. Slow, sometimes stumbling walks to perform my bodily functions with my guardian, my mom, right beside me, a great example of unconditional love that has sustained the both of us for over 15 years. I am not quite ready to make the journey away from her just yet. My work here is not quite finished.

It all started in 1987. I was filled with excitement and anticipation. The time was finally here to become reunited with my human. Everything depended on where she was; her being ready to accept a furry companion and the right canine combination. It was already determined that my human wanted a small, female dog. So, my dream of coming back as a Rottweiler was scrapped.

Next choice was a dachsund, but knew my human liked terriers. So, I had to find a situation where there was a combination of the two breeds. **AHA! Finally!** Along came a longhaired dachsund romancing with a Skye Terrier.

VOILA! The results were perfect and I was able to hold on to the colorings of the Rotty I had wanted to be and the bravado of one that would carry me through some interesting adventures with my human.

Getting into my human's life was another story. Animals know whom they belong to. There is constant documentation of how two species make the connection. My human agent was going to be her son, Eric. He had been slowly trying to convince his mom that she needed a dog. Time was of the essence. My window of opportunity was getting smaller and into the world I came, ready or not.

As it happens in the human world, unwanted puppies often find themselves in a cruel, scary environment and either taken to the Animal Control Center or just dumped. I was dumped, right in the middle of an apartment complex parking lot, scared and cold. It was the first 30-degree night of that year in Gainesville, Florida and I wandered around the complex crying my heart out, looking for my human that I was supposed to be with!

Thank goodness, for the wonderful woman, Gwen, who rescued me, took me into her nice, warm home and to work the next day, where everyone made a fuss over me. They didn't know what to do with me, so followed the normal procedure of calling the humane center, vets and even ran an ad thinking someone would claim me.

Eric took me home. **"YES"!** I was getting closer to my human. I could feel it. A meeting was set up for his mom to come and meet me. We were already communicating.

As she was driving to meet me, thinking of names for me. I was able to let her know what I wanted to be named. **"Samantha"** Yes! She got it! She was here! I could feel it! She walked in and it was love at first sight. I kissed her nose. She took me into her hands and kissed me. I shook all over with delight and peed in her hands. A habit I had a bit of a problem with the first couple of months of life a situation not unusual for puppies. I made it! I was where I belonged! I was with my human! I was ecstatically happy!

Samantha 2 1/2 months old

If you talk to animals, they will talk to you.
Chief Dan George

2

Communication

It doesn't take psychic ability to talk to us. It isn't rocket science. Animal species already have the gift. The purpose of this book is to help you develop this vital gift of communication, intuition, hunch and awareness.

Carol Gurney states in her book *The Language of Animals—7 Steps to Communicating with Animals*, "that communication and intuition is a psychic muscle which needs development and constant use. Heart is the core center. Heart to heart is not spoken it is felt. It is warm, full of love, an emotional, opening up to the spiritual. The animal does the same. Communication. Heart to Heart. Knowingness. State of receptivity. We share this with others like us and it helps create a greater intimacy."

It is important to quit telling us, or just talking at us. You need to hear and listen. Don't try to constantly reason. Let go. Just be. Develop a true balance. Slow down and ground yourself. Get rid of distractions. Loud noises, loud music, quick or darting movements are a **"no, no"**. Please understand that we are sensitive. Please consider our needs.

You've Already Been Communicating With Us

Pictures create thoughts Duhhhh..! We communicate with each other through thought. Haven't you noticed when you think of giving us a bath, depending on our perception of liking a bath or not, most of us suddenly disappear? Pictures are stronger than words.

When I was very ill and having trouble eating or being tempted by food, mom was distraught on what to feed me. Her friend, Trish, also very intuitive and somewhat objective to my needs at this time, was open mentally for me to send a picture of what I was craving.

A **HOTDOG!** I kept picturing a **"hot dog".** Trish caught the picture and told mom. Guess what. I got my hot dog, all warmed up, in tiny bite size that I could manage and sooo yummy.

I do this constantly and mom knows when I want something, need help, want to go outside, or just want to be held in her arms and communicate with her. We do our best communicating when we sit quietly on our porch swing. We exchange love kisses and mom quietly talks about the good times we've had; how important I am to her; what a great squirrel and lizard chaser I was and how much she loves me.

I look into her eyes while she talks and give little kisses on her nose and we are in our cocoon of "**heart love**". Then, my dang bladder presses in on me and I have to break our reverie to pee. Getting old can be such a pain.

The greatest part of our happiness depends
on our dispositions, not our circumstances.
Martha Washington

Attitudes and Emotions

Boy, do we pick up on those. Your attitudes, stress, any emotion even when not directed toward us. So, you can imagine what we pick up when they are zoning into our space. We're affected by your feelings and when you project them strongly to us, whether it's dismay or joy, we react.

Stressful emotions create stressful conditions inside our hearts. Too much stress can create such inner turmoil for us that can manifest behavior problems or illnesses. If you project pictures and feelings of safety, we become peaceful and quiet. Agitation, stress, anger can make us fearful, agitated and stressed as well.

DO NOT BE CONDESCENDING!!

Animals Do Remember Past Events and Can Carry Anger, Sadness and All Other Feelings

Most species carry centuries of behavior for survival and natural needs. Inbred genetic factors, veterinarian research and examinations can help you understand why we feel the way we do and what must be done to help us fit into human society. Orientation methods will help to desensitize these traits along with training, nutrition, homeopathy and understanding.

Honor our rightness.
Do not impose your attitude, ideas and viewpoint on us.
Respect us and allow us to be who we are.
Have our best interest at heart.
Don't make us feel threatened.
Some of us use words depending on how we were
communicated with from childhood on.
Try to get your own opinions and attitudes out of the way.
See us for total interpretation.
We become a mirror of your emotions.

Orientation Method

If an animal is frightened, disoriented or anxious, help point out objects to him one-by-one and point with your finger. This will help him focus. Go object to object. Repeat and move his head toward the object, gently 5-10 times and let him respond. When okay, thank him for working with you. Walk him around new objects. It helps in a new environment, such as moving. This is especially important when dealing with an elderly animal with hearing and vision loss. Always praise and thank the animal for his cooperation. This helps him to cooperate with you again.

Orientating Cats

This can be more difficult. Cats can feel out of sync—losing space around their bodies when moved suddenly. Explain everything before the move beforehand. Picture and describe the difference and what they will like about the new place.

3

Meditation

Artistic people communicate in the creative field like Creative Visualization, Images and Thoughts. Animals often send images regarding Thought, Emotion or Sensation. Practice by projecting an idea—i.e., food, ball playing, taking a walk in your mind. Ask a question, then reverse roles with your animal. See it through our perception. When we are resistant, back off and give us physical and emotional space. This often helps to let us approach you. Respect our privacy and feelings of embarrassment. See how we feel about other animals and humans. How we feel when talked about.

FOCUS—Keep a light attitude. Make it fun. Imagine sending a feeling or picture to your animal wherever he is in the room. Breathe quietly. Stay calm. Distractions **must be eliminated**. Concentrate your energy directly to the animal. With practice, you will realize you are receiving pictures and feelings back from your animal. We are naturally spiritual, more in touch with nature and not distracted by rational thought. We don't concern ourselves with tomorrow. We live in the **NOW...**Any mental, emotional, physical spiritual technique is great. Practice and see which one works best for you. **Your comfort zone is important. Remember, thought, emotion, visual, feelings all must be conveyed with clarity and one message at a time.**

Some of you just know! Trust your gut feeling. Trust the first response you receive from your animal, even if it doesn't make sense. This isn't meant to be a struggle. Humans make everything so difficult. Trust yourself. Open yourself to our projection. You are more than likely communicating with your animal without realizing and placing it on imagination. **NOT SO!** Practice, practice, and more practice. Be respectful. Ask if we are ready and if it's a good time. When ready, ask simple questions that can be validated. This builds your confidence. There is no right or wrong answer to your questions to us. Get out of your mind and talk to us. Leave logic out of this. Be still. Just be and feel. Be non-threatening or judgmental. We may make contact with you on the first try. Be quiet and receptive to us. Have constant interaction with us. Don't expect us to be conversationalists when you haven't taken time to communicate with us in any way. We are all different. Learning to listen to us will help you hear and listen to your human friends and family. Most humans do not know how to become still and listen to us, to other humans or even themselves.

Meditation Preparation

1. Physically and mentally relax, put on some soft quiet music, concentrate on breathing quietly and slowly. Become still.
2. Meditation is vital. Get rid of distractions. Create your own atmosphere and environment. Form an island of stillness. A tape on relaxation may help. Be alone. Sit in a comfortable chair, place feet firmly on the floor. Start a few minutes at a time. Concentrate on breathing.
3. Get into your heart vibration. Feel the unconditional love emanating.

Meditation to Open Your Heart Recipe

1. Breathe in to the count of 4 through your nose.

2. Hold count to the count of 4.

3. Exhale to the count of 4 through your mouth.

4. Do nothing for the count of 3.

5. Repeat.

1. Breathing is the secret of successful meditation. When practicing the above recipe, close your eyes and picture your breath coming in through your nose and going out of you mouth. As you breathe picture your body slowly relaxing. Continuing breathing, working out tension and stress points in your body. Sit comfortably. You can change position as you are doing this. Keep your eyes closed. You will slowly notice your body relaxing and feeling lighter.

As you feel the stress release and your body relax, go to the next step. Picture your very favorite place that you go to when you daydream. It may be the seashore where you hear the gentle waves slowly caressing the sand. It may be the mountains where it is cool and relaxing or a wonderful garden with a large, graceful tree gently moving in the breeze. Go there mentally, keep breathing slowly and feel your relaxation deepen as you enjoy the peace in your favorite place. Let your relaxation deepen, feel the gentle waves from the sea, float among on the clouds. Breathe quietly and effortlessly.

2. Feel the inner peace. Feel the love growing within you. Feel your inner beauty. Now picture your animal and see what your animal sees and feels from you. Feel his love slowly moving toward you.

3. Stay in this peaceful place for a few minutes. Take a few breaths and feel yourself become aware of your present environment. Slowly count from one to five, pause and open your eyes.

4. You will be experiencing a deep feeling of peace and relaxation. In this tranquil state you are now able to sit down and focus on your animal.

5. Let go of distractions. Feel yourself centered. If distracted and confused, stop and slow your breathing and start over. Remember, the secret is quiet, slow, even breathing. Be repetitive and childlike. Put a picture in your mind and slowly project it mentally to your animal. Be slow and methodical when doing this. Pictures create thoughts. Be realistic. It may seem difficult at first. There may still be some mind clutter and mind noise, but it lessens as you practice. Relaxation techniques and breathing will get you there.

6. Keep the picture and command to your animal simple. Keep the mind chatter down. Send a message for the animal to come to you. Send a picture of the animal obeying your command and see him getting up from where he is. Repeat the command mentally one more time and wait. The animal might respond or may seem confused. That's all right. Stop and give your animal hugs, kisses and verbal appreciation. Try again another day and you will eventually have success, giving you and your pet a new opening to start more communication with wonderful results. Practice makes perfect.

7. Be in the moment. Enjoy that feeling. Living in the now and in the moment will make an animal's emotions more powerful and more stable than human emotions.

Intuitive Development

Intuition is what the brain knows what to do when you leave it alone. Dr. Paul MacLean

Intuitive development is so important. Intuition and telepathy is the native tongue of all animal species. Intuitive touch and massaging methods work best. Again, acknowledge your animal to be able to open up the area where energy needs to be manipulated and he will learn to look forward to your gentle touch. Be open to all methods of healing and use other healers when needed. Pay attention to telepathic thought and energy from your animal. This will tell you if he is responding favorably to your continuing or becoming edgy or restless telling you to stop. Talk to him acknowledging you received his message.

Spiritual

It is important for you to be or to become spiritual to share deep communication with us. Communication is achieved through important clarity of thought, pictures and feelings. Sense our mental and spiritual qualities, thoughts and essence as a being. Feel in close content with it. Experiment different types of communicating with us. See which works best.

My mom and I used all methods based on simple words, pictures and feelings. As I grew up, my vocabulary became profound. I had mastered simple sentences. We could never understand the amazement of our human friends at my understanding mom's requests and comments to me.

Geez! She even managed to train and communicate with the cats in our lives! Even when they acted like "**Such Cats**".

The past three years, even with failing eyesight and hearing, I can still hear mom's thoughts and pictures in my mind. I obey most of the time. But, not hearing much, has its advantages. I've slowed down tremendously. Our 10 minute walk now takes 30 minutes and I'm left off the leash much of the time as a result. Hey, how much trouble can a 15yo, shuffling, plodding mutt get into?

Mom stops to chat with her neighbor friend and I just ignore her calling me, pretending I can't hear at all or feel her message. I can feel her laughing and know she will catch up to me with a couple of giant strides with her long, long legs. Darn! Next life I'm coming back as a 6' tall human. I love to watch mom stretch those long, long legs. It doesn't take much to catch up to me, I'm short stuff remember? Only 8" high at the shoulder and with my age, have probably shrunk a bit. She catches up to me and gently guides me, making sure I stay on the path and we slowly amble along, stopping every so often.

I have to stop and smell who's been out that day and mom looks at the sky, drinking in the peace and beauty into her soul. I know what she sees. I don't have to look. I receive her mind pictures and feel the food from her soul enter mine. We continue our walk. **We are still good for each other.**

Telepathy

Don't try and push too hard. When you quit pushing and trying to figure something out, the answer is suddenly there.

Example: My mom is constantly losing her keys, glasses and phone. I personally think it is something genetic with humans. She will run around frantically, praying to St. Anthony (patron saint of lost articles) and out of exasperation finally sits down to breathe and become still. A thought (picture, i.e., behind the couch) comes into her mind. She gets up, goes to that place and dang if that missing item isn't there. You understand of course, who sent her the thought (picture) of where to look, don't you? **MOI!** It soon becomes apparent to her that these messages are flowing to her from me.

Is she any better in not losing her keys, glasses and phone? **Heck NO!** She still hollers for St. Anthony and then sits for a quiet moment, waiting for me to send her the picture of where she last placed the missing item **Cheeze.** You wonder who the caretaker in this home is? **MOI! that's who!** Our cat Sati, could care less. She just looks at mom with disdain and goes back doing her cat thing. The lesson here is to relax and breathe. You humans run around hyper-ventilating constantly and your brain doesn't get enough oxygen.

Remember, this isn't Rocket Science. It's about Just Being and learning patience. Keep things simple. Simple words, simple thoughts. We don't appreciate a lot of blathering. Makes us tune you out. Images. We function on images, pictures, thoughts.

Again, let's reiterate. My mom loses her keys, starts to pace frantically. looking in all the wrong places. She finally sits down. Do you think I walk over to her saying, "Excuse me madam, let's stop a moment and ponder on who, what and where your keys may have gone?"

Trash all the nonsense words. I intuitively know when her breathing has calmed down her mental train wreck and quickly, telepathically project a picture of where she last lay her keys. **Simple, simple, simple.** Humans make work of the most apparent solutions. It exhausts me to think about it. Receive and trust information. No need to interpret. Preconceived ideas interfere with actual responses. You are not listening. Be receptive. Detach from your feelings.

Doubting

Do not be intimidated. Be patient with yourself and your animal. As time goes on with practice, communication will become clearer and accurate. Embrace your own technique. Develop it. Quit being logical. Feel by asking a question. Need clarification? Ask for it. Keep it simple.

My mom and I have conversations. They started with mom directing a picture to me, often associating it with a word, i.e., the picture of me peeing. Mom would transmit the picture to me, when we were outside, using the word "hurry". Job #2 was also associated with her picturing me in that position and saying "hurry, hurry".

The continuous usage of the same word for certain functions kept confusion away. In that manner I learned to obey certain commands i.e., sit and stay. Little by little my vocabulary became enhanced. Mom used words and simple sentences with a picture of what she was saying transmitted to me verbally and telepathically.

Granted, I am a highly intelligent and very evolved member of my species. But believe me, you too can develop conversation with your animal species. Just keep it simple. Be patient and gentle. Ask us for help. Flow into our world. Let us pull you into our world. **DO NOT try to lunge into us. That is scary and rude.** You will hit a brick wall and we will totally retreat from you. Take a time-out. Regroup. Apologize and try the correct way later when your animal becomes more responsive and trusting.

4

Choosing an Animal

In order to keep a true perspective
of one's importance,
everyone should have a dog that worships him
and a cat that ignores you.
Dereke Bruce

Don't crowd the house with other animals. Talk to us first. We may have chosen to live with you to lead a solitary life when you are at work or away. If we feel the need for companionship, after talking to us and getting our approval, please, let us look over the candidate. Let us talk with them to see if they will fit into our lifestyle. Remember, those of us in your household first, become the elder, the leader, unless we wish to relinquish it to the newcomer. Don't hurt our feelings. We were here first. When coming home from work or wherever, follow protocol. Make sure to greet us first—then greet the new addition to the family. Do you like to be ignored? Neither do we.

Play with us as before. We want our own toys. Newcomers need to have their own. We will then decide among ourselves if we choose to share or not. Avoid anything that will make us feel threatened. Humans aren't the only ones with fears and insecurities, we have them as well. You are not the only members of that club. Give us separate areas at first. Please. For eating, sleeping and for gosh sakes, more than one cat? then—more than one litter box PUHLEEZ! Maintain a relationship with your first pets. Separate play-time, eating dishes, etc. Give us a sense of importance and belonging. Do not take us for granted.

Use telepathy to choose an animal. Ask us what our wishes are, especially when bringing a new animal into the home. We have strong feelings about whom we wish to live with.

Mom, bless her heart, respected that. She and I sat down and talked about having another dog come live with us. After visiting the local Humane Society a few times, mom narrowed the choices down to two that she felt could fit into our home life comfortably, a Highland White Terrier and Border Collie mix. Which one did she choose? She didn't. I did. I escorted her to the Humane Society and in a small yard setting, they were brought out to us, one at a time.

The Border Collie came out first. I said **NO**. It became immediately apparent that there would be competition for mom's attention. Next came the Highland White Terrier. Gadzoots! What an emotional, nervous wreck he was. He cried like a baby. I knew I had my work cut out for me, but he touched my heart. Mom was a little shocked and dismayed at my choice, but honored it. He was such a wimp that we named him Rambo, hoping the tough-guy name would help give him a touch of confidence. It took work and reinforcement on my part to help him through some really difficult times and it paid off.

The really rough part came in dealing with his abandonment issue. He was purchased by college students as a puppy. Taught some really weird habits, like shrieking at the top of his lungs when someone came home. This habit almost drove my mom deaf and crazy. He was abandoned in an empty apartment for around five days before found. Then he was locked up in the animal shelter for over two weeks.

When mom found him, he was on the schedule to be euthanized. His time was up for taking needed room at the shelter. Like I said, he had problems. But we hung in there and worked through most of them.

We are here to love and be loved.
We are your animal children.
Carol Gurney

Responsibility

You are taking us on for life. Not to play with and get rid of when we're grown, going through some trials with behavior or health and to be treated with respect and care during our senior years.

This is not to be taken lightly. We come into your life for mutual development. We love you unconditionally and without restraint. Your mission when taking us into your home and life is to care for us in every responsible way and to learn patience and love from us.

This is a spiritual journey. We will not desert you or hold love and affection from you. If you abuse us, desert us, treat us as non-entities without a soul, I am here to tell you that you are building up karma (cause and effect) that will have to be taken care of in this lifetime or another lifetime.

Our Job and Mission

All of us, humans and animal species have a job and mission in life. Mom called me her "**little politician and official greeter**". A very auspicious position, let me tell you. I was a **"schmoozer".** I would roll my **"baby browns"** and the most aloof person would be won over.

Perks were pretty good with this position as well. I was allowed in areas closed off to all dogs, snacks aplenty and tons of praise and appreciation for my talents and beauty. When I thought a meeting or get-together with friends started to lag, I would get things rolling by spitting a racquet ball into the middle of the group hollering **"PLAY BALL".** That always got action and hilarity going. I was invited to many homes and events.

As I became older, I would sit in the living room and share knowledge with mom and her friends. I would come out from my favorite resting area, make myself known, make my presence felt, say hello, visit and go back to rest. Remember mom's friends are highly intuitive, so I could still hear the conversations and pictures they were saying and projecting and they picked up my thoughts. This is definitely where familiarity was comfortable.

Let us know you appreciate us and appreciate our help and positions we hold in your life. As we get older, help release us from our obligations of being a caretaker. Work on keeping yourself emotionally balanced as well.

The secret of success is consistency of purpose.
Benjamin Disraeli...

Images, Pictures and Thoughts

Again, here's the trick. Simplify your thoughts. Too many times you are sending..."Do this...don't do that...but darn, they'll do it again, right after I say not to". **HALLOOO!** One thought at a time. You get us confused with your mixed signals and thoughts. Just because you are having a train wreck in your mind, doesn't mean you have to send one to us. **SIMPLIFY!**

A picture of the outdoors suddenly calls out to you. You look up and see your dog gazing longingly out the window or pacing near the door, wanting to go out. A picture of a water bowl flashes across your mind. You follow your intuitive picture flash and find the water bowl empty and your animal walking away from it. Pictures, images, thoughts, all the same thing.

My mom house trained me that way. I would feel her looking at me and a picture of me peeing on the green grass came into my mind's eye. Next thing to happen? PICTURE, CAMERA, ACTION! My mom was suddenly running out the door carrying me while I was happily peeing. Her picture that she sent, gave me such a warm feeling that I just couldn't help it. Needless to say mom learned real fast. She made sure I was actually on the grass before she pictured me peeing.

It's a matter of semantics of who trains whom.
Keep it simple and we both learn
how to communicate with each other.

Some images transmitted from your animal come in slow motion and you must stay very still as the picture becomes clear (like a Polaroid). Be careful of your thoughts around us. Remember we use telepathy and see and hear what your thoughts are. We ignore your blathering and train wrecks in your mind. However, thoughts, i.e., you want us out of your life, wish us dead,. have overwhelming effects making us depressed, and fearful of our lives. Self-esteem becomes harmed and often illnesses can result.

Let us be who we are
Be present in every moment.
Live today. Live in the now
Ask our viewpoint
Acknowledge us and our feelings.
Let us in on the information. Don't assume.

Hey, we also understand time. I know when mom is coming back from store, etc.. She tells me verbally and with pictures what she is going to do and the approximate time she will be back. This is relayed to me even when asleep and I receive the message. Hey, we're asleep, not in a coma and you keep forgetting we receive messages telepathically. I don't get fretful as a result and am up waiting to greet her to see what kind of goodies she brought back.

We also know how old we are. You don't have to rub it in. We realize our faculties are changing and are becoming impaired. I lose my balance at times and mom quickly assesses the situation to see if I can get up by myself or need assistance. Leave it to my mom, she clucks like a mother hen, making the appropriate noises without making me lose face and be embarrassed over the mishap. I appreciate her so much that I told her that since I am coming back as a human in my next life, if she would like to come back as a dog, I would take wonderful, loving care of her the way she took care of me.

Work is either fun or drudgery..
It depends on your attitude.
I like fun.
Colleen C. Barrett

Colors

There is an ongoing debate on whether we can or cannot see color. Here we go again. I realize what scientists say and the common belief is that dogs lack cones responsible for color reception within our eyes. Truth or fiction? How do you explain how we're affected by color?

I had definite favorite colors. I loved Smiley Face latex balls in green. I nosed around with the lavender and yellow balls, and would play "keep away and chase" with the **green** ones. I wouldn't play with yellow ones and adored blue racquet balls. Those were for roughhouse playing where I would do a lot of barking, running and throwing it back to mom to throw again.

I feel that I see color. I always noticed when mom changed her haircut or changed the color of her hair. I loved it when we were color coordinated with our cool weather garments. I wore my lavender sweater and mom her lavender sweatshirt. People noticed and would smile and comment on our sense of style. It always made me feel proud and it showed in my prancing and strutting walk. And, if you notice, thoughts and pictures sent back and forth between us are also in color. So who is right? Does it really make a difference? Perhaps not, but watch the toys we pick to play with and ones that we ask you to buy when we go shopping with you in pet stores.

We grow in time to trust the future for our answers.
Longfellow

Time and Information

No one enjoys life without knowing what each day will bring. What makes you think we are different? You make decisions for us, giving us a feeling of being powerless, not being part of the family. You expect us to constantly accept. Yes, we pick up thoughts, but remember most of you have constant train wrecks in your mind, making it impossible to even think of, much less figure out. Would it hurt you to talk to us? Give us an approximation of when to expect you home? Consideration is needed here. We do know and understand time. Research has been done on that. There have been many books written on the subject.

My mom had to make a trip out of state and she carefully explained what she would be doing and why. She made sure I had a caring person to tend to my needs and playtime. I don't like to be alone at night.

All was well until mom arrived to her destination, then I lost mental contact with her. I became afraid. I thought something happened, or she left me forever. I didn't know she had taken ill and went into deep meditation to rejuvenate herself and was cutting her trip short. As a result, she arrived home the next evening. I was so relieved, but with feelings still hurt, wouldn't greet or kiss her at first.

Mom, being mom, wouldn't take no for an answer. She quietly petted me, cooing her sweet noises to me, coaxing me to her. She sat, ignoring her friends that drove her home from the airport and told me of her trip. How sick she had become. How much she missed me. How much she loved me.

Did I stay angry? Am I stupid? **NO WAY!** I gave up my foolishness and loved her back. Part of my hurt feelings was because I wasn't included in her journey. I wanted to go with her. I know my health condition and age stops me from accompanying mom many places anymore. Yes, I am very aware of my age. Aware that my life cycle is nearing completion. That is one reason I want my wonderful human constantly near me.

Our roles have completely reversed. When young, I watched and protected my human. Comforted her in times of crises and sadness. I still perform the duty of making her take breaks out of her busy day by going for a stroll. The young days were filled with energetic playing, much laughter, gayety and love. The days are now filled with reflection, quiet appreciation, soft laughter and still with love.

We had a crises when I was recently very ill and both mom and I suffered because of it. We both knew I was very ill and a conventional vet was necessary. What happened later was unforgivable and the fault of the vet.

I needed blood work and mom explained to me that I had to stay at the vet's and would be picked up in a few hours. The vet was more than competent but thoroughly disorganized and I won't go into detail why. The result was, the blood work wasn't completed and at close of day, they called mom and said the test was very necessary and had to be done that evening in order for the results to be in the following morning. Neither one of us slept that night. Mom was anguished and angry. I was very frightened for many reasons.

Now remember, mom and I have wonderful, developed telepathic powers for each other. I finally felt her calming down sending me pictures of being back in her arms the next morning and going home. As a result, I finally fell asleep, somewhat restless, but holding on to the picture of being back home and safe.

Explain trips your animal will take. If the vet is too stupid and insensitive to fully explain the procedures to both you and your animal, change vets.

Needless to say, mom's not taking me back to this hyperkinetic, completely disorganized man, though very competent as I said. He did give me the right medication, but his energy leads to constant train wrecks and incapability of communicating with humans and as a result animals.

Do not take this responsibility lightly.
We are not toys.
We are species with feelings.
We are species with a soul.
Put yourself in our paws.

5

Behavior Problems

Potty Training

Never stand between a dog and the hydrant.
John Peers

Don't degrade us by hitting us or rubbing our noses into our accidents. You may have missed the first integral steps needed in our training. (Refer to the chapter on Images, Pictures and Thoughts and how I was trained.) You missed a very important step in training us to let you know when we want or need to go out.

Simple communication can in most cases solve behavior problems. It is unfortunate we have to go to such bizarre methods to let you know that something is not "kosher" with us. Once we've been checked by the vet and given a clean bill of health, it is apparent that there is something-emotional going on. Let me give you an example.

When I was two years old, my mom got very sick and was rushed to the emergency room without any explanation to me on what was going on. She had a couple of friends stop by and care for me during her hospital stay. Again, with all the confusion, there was lack of communication on what was happening.

I was used to sleeping with her. I was scared and lonely. I was home alone for two nights. Was there fear and concern? YES! This was my mom, my guardian, the human that I came from the spirit world to be with to spend my dog years with. I became more and more frightened and insecure. By the time mom came home on the third day, I was a trembling basket case. Happy? Yes, gloriously happy, but still so frightened, very insecure and very angry!

Mom was working on putting our lives back in order, but I was acting up. When she left for work I was afraid she would be gone for days again and leave me. I was acting out my anger and letting her know by leaving traces of my defiance on the Dining Room floor. There weren't accusations pointed at me, just the question of Why. She just wasn't getting the message, so I kept leaving the messages.

After the fourth day of picking up my presents, mom sat down on the floor, looked deeply into my eyes with love and concern and said **"OK, you've gotten my attention. Please tell me what is wrong".** I sat there in front her, not moving, just staring back into her eyes and her heart. She continued saying **"You're angry with me and afraid".** I cocked my head to let her know I was listening and sending more messages.

Her conversation continued..."**You were confused. Worried about what happened. You were afraid being left alone, not knowing where I was and you are showing me your anger and fear".** My whole body was quivering with excitement. She knew. She knew how I was feeling. She wasn't angry.

I wanted to jump into her arms, but held myself back. I needed one more thing. We continued looking at each other and our hearts touched. Mom apologized for leaving me so suddenly and alone and promised that would never happen again. There would always be someone with me through the night and that I would always know what was happening. That was what I needed. The recognition of the message I was sending and an apology. Our hearts connected. We were back on track. Needless to say, there was much joyful hugging and kisses and no more gifts left by me because of simple communication. Are you surprised? Why? When will you quit treating us as a sub-species? We are intelligent and I daresay, usually more intelligent than humans. It is proven constantly.

That same year, mom had another hospital stay, this time for a few days. Was I nervous and a bit frightened? Of course! Remember, this is my mom, my human that I am meant to be with. Was there a repetition of the past behavior problem? Absolutely not! Why? Because mom talked to me carefully about her leaving for a few days and assured me that our friend Susan would stay with me the whole time she was gone.

Susan and I were friends...Her nickname for me was "**Cocktail Wienie**" said with humorous love. In fact Susan knew how much mom and I were missing each other and was going to sneak me into the hospital as a visitor. As it turned out, mom was released that particular afternoon and I had complete happiness once again.

A problem is not always resolved on the first try. We can develop bad habits. Something we have in common with humans. The key words here are repetition and patience. Habits take time to break. You should know that.

To err is human. To forgive is Canine.
Unknown

Too many of us have been euthanized because of misunderstood behavior. Aggressive behavior needs to be addressed with a complete physical from the vet and patience and communication from you. Too often aggressiveness is misinterpreted. It is a call for help.

Again, it's not rocket science. It is taking time to be still and communicate telepathically with mental pictures and talking to us. Unless there is an organic health issue, it is emotional and sorry to say, but you, the human are the culprit and reason for our behavior problem. Straighten out your thinking, actions, stress, attitudes and how you relate to us and the behavior problem will go away. We are not your punching bags for your personal situations and difficulties. We are here to teach and love one another.

It is our desire to please you.

All animals know that the ultimate of life is to enjoy it.
Samuel Butler

Agitation and Stress

Agitation and stress is manifested very often in our behavior. It is imperative to find out the cause. Relaxation methods are helpful. Breathing and Tellington TTouch help in stressful situations. Let your animal hear your deep breathing. This helps us relax and we will begin to breathe with you. Talk gently and quietly. When relaxed, we may allow you to touch us. Learning the Tellington TTouch method is a plus for both you and your animal. This book is listed in the Bibliography Section in the last pages.

Alternative therapies, such as acupuncture, acupressure, massage, herbal and homeopathy work well. Many animal communicators, natural vets and trainers use Bach Flower Remedies, Telling TTouch and energy work. There are suggested books in the Bibliography section. Bach Rescue Remedy is a popular remedy, relaxing distressed, agitated animals and can be found in most health and vitamin stores. There are various ways of administering this product.

The most popular way is to apply 3-5 drops of the Rescue Remedy to the animal's drinking water. Other animals in the house will also benefit from the relaxing properties in this remedy. You can also dilute two drops in a tablespoon of water, or administer four drops directly to their food.

I was petrified of storms and mom would just put two drops directly into my mouth and would administer it every 10 minutes for a total of four times. This helped if it was a long, ferocious storm, or if it took me that long to relax. Usually after the second dose, I would just relax against her and go to sleep, not caring what was going on outside.

In extreme cases of distress, this can be administered four times per day or every 5-8 minutes in times of crisis. Rescue Remedy has helped both mom and me through some very critical issues when I became ill. Mom also used it for herself. That helped her focus directly on the problem and not feel like there was a train wreck in her mind and heart. These dosages were given upon the approval of my wonderful homeopathic doctor.

When dealing with an animal that is agitated or stressed, talk gently and quietly. When your pet is relaxed, he might allow you to touch him. Find out the cause from your pet. Continue the communication to move forward with any additional needs he may have. Again, remember, patience, repetition and time are key factors.

Dogs come when they're called.
Cats take a message and get back to you later.
Mary Bly

Fear of Abandonment

There are exceptions to fear of abandonment, but this type of behavior usually affects those of us who have had no inter-social skills with other animals or humans. This behavior is also with those of us who have developed a co-dependency on a human. We need other animal friends, human friends, meeting others of our species on walks in the neighborhood or parks.

I fortunately didn't have that problem. From the day I was brought together with my human, I had constant interaction with other humans and other animals. I was involved in everything.

I was a "party girl". I was included in get-togethers, dinners and parties that my mom would have or go to. I traveled with her to visit friends and family. I was the **"hostess with the mostest".** I would run to the door greeting everyone with joyful barking, welcoming their arrival. Ours was a home where other animal friends were welcome, giving me hours of playtime and some doggie conversation and gossip. People loved me and I loved people. I was a true diplomat. Life was great!!

My dog thinks he's human.
My cat thinks he is God.
unknown

Cats Cannot Be Trained

Whenever mom hears that comment, she just throws her head back, roars with laughter and says "Rubbish". This female human trained all three cats that lived with her.

Two of the cats, Rhubarb and Taii, were raised together. Being cats, there were many squabbles, but they knew when boundaries had been overstepped and mom's last nerve was pushed. There were days you would walk into the house and see each cat on a separate beanbag going through a time out.

People would laugh, not believing their eyes or ears when one or both were being disciplined for some infraction. All mom had to do was let out a type of growl, point her finger and they would freeze in motion. Taii would carry it one step further and roll over on his back with his legs in the air crying "**uncle**".

Taii

Sati, her present cat is another good example. We have a lovely patio and Sati is allowed on it with instructions to not jump the fence. Being a normal cat, the temptation was too great and over she went. **Lawdie.,** when mom discovered her gone, I ran under the bed. I didn't want to witness what might transpire. Mom opened the garden gate, let out a ferocious growl and Sati came running home like her tail was on fire.

Then it started, mom caught and held her Sati's entire body close to her body, looked into her eyes and said very loudly, enunciating each word to alleviate any misunder-standing, **"you are grounded, you are not allowed on the patio for a week".** Sati joined me under the bed, breathing hard, heart pounding and frightened. She wasn't sure if there was more punishment to follow or not. Our human however, doesn't believe in physical punishment. She gets our attention with noises, growls and saying our name with a disapproving tone in her voice.

Sati, however, is an example of having to get a point across more than once to break a habit. This is very normal for a cat. Most cats feel the urge to be **"wild and free",** especially when being the offspring of a feral mother. Such was the case with Sati and the **"urge to roam, to be free"** hit once again and over the fence she flew. Mom just happened to see her in motion and like a flashing bullet went after her. A sound resembling a tornado came out of mom's mouth. Sati froze in mid-air, made a complete 180 degree turn and her entire body was caught before she hit the ground.

I never want to get such a tongue lashing or hear such anger directed toward me. After a lecture on the dangers, diseases and predators lurking out here for helpless cats, mom then sentenced Sati to being grounded for two weeks with window privileges also taken away. After the two weeks were up, Sati was once again allowed on the patio. When she hears her name said softly, she bounds into the house like the **"headless horseman"** is coming after her. Her curiosity is still there. After all she is a cat.

Sati

God created domestic cats so that
men might touch tigers.
D.A.N.

Moving

When changing location of residence, talk to us. Communicate with us. Don't expect us to read your minds at a time like that. Your minds are a train wreck with worries and anxieties over the move. Talk to us quietly with positive images. Tell us when we will move. We are aware of time—remember?

Explain to us how you will handle us during that time. Where will you put us to keep us safe and when will you come to pick us up? Describe the new place. Send thoughts and pictures of each room, the outdoors. How will we get there? How long will the trip take to get there? Do your research on practical, safe tips for a safe and happy move with us included. Take time to talk to us. Reassure us. Listen to our thoughts and questions. This will insure a happy, calm adjustment to a new place for all concerned.

A little Bach Rescue Remedy in our water, starting about a month before the move and about a month after the move will help lower the stress. There are further tips to help make the moving transition and orientation that can be researched and books to read. Check the Bibliography area of the book. Give us time, usually two to four weeks to adapt. Work with us. Be patient and calm. The effort will be worth it.

Sati, our 10 year old cat species is a very good example of being a very relaxed cat in most environments, moves and trips. She loves car travel. Mom would talk to her about the trip we were taking, place her in a carrier, adjust her firmly in the center of the back seat in order for her to see out the front window and have communication with the both of us. I traveled on the front passenger seat on top of pillows, strapped in with a safety harness to the seat belt. We traveled in comfort and safety.

Sati would ask more questions of where we were going and how long it would take. After hearing mom's answers, she would just curl up and go to sleep until we arrived at our destination.

The same thing was done during our resident moves. Sati would be told about what was happening, along with me of course, and placed in her carrier, to keep her out of harm's way, and off we would go to a new place, a new adventure without all of the problems that most humans run into with their animals. Sati was so comfortable with these transitions, that she was even very comfortable when Michael, a friend of ours, took her in his car to what ended up being my last place to move to with them. She ended up bonding very closely on the ride with Michael and to this day, they still remain the closest of buddies.

Why was the transaction so smooth? Because our human always takes time to talk to us and explain what is happening. We don't have to become insecure and afraid that we will be left behind, forgotten or mistreated. Communication is constant in our home between the three of us, and anyone that is a friend of ours as well. We are treated with respect, love and consideration. We are a happy family.

6

Lost

Never give up, Never, ever, ever, ever..
Churchill

It can be a matter of life and death to learn to communicate with us. Things happen. Disasters occur. Storms happen. Fire, floods, all manner of tragedies and non-tragedies.

I know first hand about this kind of danger. I got temporarily in trouble. Being dachshund/terrier, I am a hunter, explorer and as humans phrase it "**just plain nosy**". I walk around with my nose to the ground, constantly sniffing, in search of treasure at the end of a spore trail.

My mom and I had just moved to Tampa, Florida and temporarily lived in a rooming house that I found fascinating. You could hear the mice scrambling inside the walls at night. I would sit for hours staring into the cold air duct on the first floor, watching and hearing the little rodents scurrying around.

I went outside for last call before bedtime and before mom grabbed the flashlight, was down the stairs into the yard and on the trail. In the blink of an eye, I was gone. I knew where I was, but forgot how I got into the space I was in.

I heard mom calling. I kept showing her mentally where I was, but her fright and not finding me immediately, blocked our telepathic channels. Problem was, the picture I was sending her was dark. I was inside the base of the chimney leading to the fireplace and it was dark with an opening a bit too high for me to jump up and get through. Remember I am only 8" high at the shoulders. So, mom kept getting a mental picture of a dark wall. I could feel her fear. I did nothing but concentrate on sending my spirit energy to her. I felt her take a deep breath and felt her pray. I took that moment to mentally say the word **"HERE".** I felt her response and movement to where I was located and could see the flashlight with its beacon coming closer. I sent the word out again. She stopped and became very still. I did it again. And suddenly there was the flashlight bouncing along the wall and it caught my eye reflection. Mom reached in, pulled me out and asked me why I didn't bark to let her know where I was. Truth was, I never thought of barking. I was too busy sending the word **"HERE".**

Sometimes, animals don't want to be found for one reason or another. Most of us do and when communication lines have been developed between the species, more happy endings can be experienced, even though it can be at times a hit and miss preposition.

Some common reasons animals get lost are from being too adventurous, frightened, chased and not paying attention to their surroundings. This is common when moved to a new location or disaster of some kind happens altering the familiar environment. Then there is the feeling that their time with a human is over, or they can be in the process of trying to find the person they are searching for in this particular lifetime.

Rambo was a perfect example of one on the search for his rightful owner. This was the wimpy, frightened, cry baby I chose when my mom took me to visit at the Humane Society shelter in Gainesville, Florida. Due to illness and mom needing an experimental drug, we moved from Florida to Knoxville, TN. Rambo and I were prepared for the trip and excited about having a new experience and adventure.

After our move, Rambo and I would work a real guilt trip on mom by sitting in the front window when she had to leave for work, throwing our heads back howling for all we were worth. Things got much more interesting however. Rambo ended up having to be leashed when let outside, because he decided to take to the hills and run away. We couldn't understand why. It seemed like he couldn't help himself. He would go out, sniff the air and the chase would be on. There he would go. Where? Who knew? He sure didn't.

Before a year passed, mom's position was terminated, health improved and we would be returning to Florida. Garage Sale time. A ritual always before moving and a part of life as I know it. This particular garage sale changed our lives and brought Rambo face-to-face with his destiny.

Mom had advertised the garage sale in a paper and a call came in from a man in the process of moving his family from S. Dakota to a burg a bit south of Knoxville and they needed things for their new home. One question from him was **"by the way, is there any chance that you have a dog you are considering finding a new home for"?** The answer of course, was **"NO",** even though mom was concerned about coming back to Florida with two dogs. It was difficult enough finding a place to accept one dog much less two.

After discussing what else there was for sale, the family came by that same day and it was mind boggling. This man walked in with three children, and a very pregnant wife. When he and Rambo saw each other, it was like velcro hit. Rambo took a flying leap and landed in this man's arms and hugging him for all he was worth. Let me tell you, everyone's mouth was hanging open and I was plain upset. What was going on? Why was Rambo so happy to see this man?

The family spent a couple of hours with us, purchasing some items they needed for the house. Rambo, in the meantime was slowly edging to the youngest child that was afraid of dogs, since one had bitten him on the foot some time back. Before you knew it, Rambo was next to this little boy and the boy was petting his head.

That did it. The man wanted Rambo. My mom tried to explain that Rambo came from an abused background where he was owned by some college students, abandoned in the apartment for a few days and then in the slammer for over two weeks before we found him. He was terrified to go down any kind of stairs and petrified to get in a car. Mom would carry him up and down the stairs and lift him into the car, trying to ease his fears. And he had the terrible habit of singing at the top of his lungs in an extremely high-pitched voice that made mom's hair stand on end. This didn't phase the man at all and when they were leaving, Rambo completely embarrassed mom by running out of the house down the stairs and jumping into the car of this family.

The family was ready to take Rambo home and mom said, **"Whoa, this is happening too fast. Let's think about this overnight."** Well, you never saw such carryings on after they left. Rambo pouted and walked around with his tail between his legs, wouldn't eat and wouldn't talk or even look at me. The next morning mom called the family and told them to come back and pick up their dog. Such happiness. Rambo found the man and family that he had been looking for. They kept in touch with mom for a short time reporting how Rambo was faring.

It seems Rambo became one of the kids, eating pizza, drinking koolaid, swimming in the river, marking his territory outside, standing protection over the family and when going to pick up the father, would sing at the top of his lungs and they loved it. They felt that was his way of telling everybody how happy he was to be with them. But, I wasn't happy. I didn't talk to mom for three weeks. It took a tremendous amount of coaxing and talking to me to try to convince me that Rambo was with his right human. I felt he was my pet and buddy. What a bummer! It took mom a bit of time to convince me that I would stay where I was with her. I was where I belonged and to be happy for Rambo, that he was able to finally quit running away trying to find the human he was set on finding when he came into this lifetime.

Rambo

This is just one example of what animals do to find their rightful guardian and human companion.

There are certain immediate, practical steps to take when an animal is gone.

- Check all organizations who help locating lost animals.

- Check with local rescuers listed in the yellow pages under Humane Society, SPCA, Pets, Pet Adoptions.
- Vet clinics, emergency vet rooms, shelters (animals can travel a long distance.) pet rescue, lost and found animals.
- Flyers with photo and telephone number.
- Ads in local papers.

When running an ad for a found animal, **do not** include the description. Limit the information. Make the person answering the ad describe the animal in full detail, gender, size, weight, color, color eyes, length of fur, distinguishing marks, personality traits, color of collar, tags, description of tag or tattoo. There are predators out there. Be sure it is the right person or family.

- Talk to neighbors, mail carriers, trash collectors, everybody that works or enters your area.
- Search party.
- Stay calm, call your pet with a reassuring voice. Use your telepathic abilities.
- Contact someone who can telepathically talk to animals.

Ask them for help or call a professional animal communicator. To increase chances finding your pet, it is important to move things along quickly. It can however, take time.

- Meditate—Visualize a beam of white light from your heart to your pet's heart. Make it a large, white beam, a strong beacon, a giant flashlight, lighting up the entire sky.

Say his name. Stay calm Keep the light on from your heart to his. This will help your pet find his way home. Go into the meditative state and use the meditation recipe described in Chapter Three.

Get comfortable. Sit with feet firmly on the ground. Close your eyes. Breathe deeply, slowly, releasing tension. Focus on your heart. Feel your love for your pet. See your pet in front of you. Then send a huge beacon of light to him from your heart to his heart. Tell him to see the light. Feel the light. It will bring him home." Tell him to "keep looking at the light. It will bring him home."

Use Your Intuition

Keep your thoughts on a positive track. No negative thoughts are allowed. Picture your pet safe, with plenty of water and food, warm, sheltered and with the white light wrapped around him like a safe cape. No fear is allowed. It scatters energy. You must stay focused to keep the connection going. It doesn't hurt to ask your angels and spirit guides for help in keeping him safe and guiding him home. When making the intuitive connection, it isn't surprising to receive information images, smells, feelings and words they may be sending. Remember that is how my human found me when I was stuck in the chimney and it was total darkness? She calmed down, started to breathe deeply and she heard me say the word **"Here".** My voice gave her direction and got stronger when she got closer to where I was. Breathing, listening, intuition and heart connection helped her find me.

Keep meditating. Keep trying. It may take your pet awhile to get his bearings. He may be afraid, disoriented, hungry, lonely, trapped or injured. Surround him with a gentle light such as a light violet to ease his anxiety. Deep breathing will calm you down and result in sending calm thoughts and calm feelings to your pet. Talk quietly and gently to him. Reassure him of your love. It may take more than one try at different intervals to make the connection. Try to accomplish this within the first 24 hours.

Once communication has been accomplished, continue it as a source of comfort and encouragement. You are now able to ask questions for your pet to give descriptions of his surroundings. **Remember, we can see colors**. What he hears, if he sees other animals or humans around there. What he sees when he looks up, when he looks down. Is he outside or inside a structure. What details stand out. Pay careful attention to every impression. Write them down. Digest the information given and trust it. Analyze it and act on it.

It is vital to have a tattoo or embedded microchip on your animal. Remember, accidents and disasters happen. This will often help reunite a lost animal with their human.

Because of fear on the part of the human and animal, it may take more than a few times to finally make contact. Space your communication techniques with a 45-minute break and try again. It sometimes takes a few hours to finally make contact, especially if there was an injury involved or sudden death. They can still be under the illusion that they are still alive and not in spirit. Also, when a traumatic injury occurs, the spirit can temporarily leave the body before realizing that it is still alive. That is referred to as **"being scared out of our mind"** making it seem as if we are no longer earth bound. Again, the key factor is to become calm, breathe deeply, meditate and intuitively communicate telepathically. Send loving, calming images and love. Connect heart to heart. Do not hesitate to ask for assistance of an animal communicator.

Job Finished

Many of us hold onto life longer than our original life-span contract for this incarnation. We do so until we are assured that our human can go on with their mission without our continued physical and spiritual help.

A good example was Taii, a gorgeous, white 17lb Tomcat that I had the privilege of living with the first two years of my life. After a few incidents of him showing me who was boss, (I still have the scar above my left eye when he grabbed my entire head into his mouth to prove it) and my tenacious persistence, we became close friends. He, at first grudgingly accepted me, then slowly tolerated me with feelings slowly developing into caring and love.

He carefully watched and noted the love and understanding between our human and me. He already had this wonderful bond with her and would watch our communication development and mishaps with amusement. His favorite place, besides the fireplace hearth was a papasan chair. It was apparent that he was becoming more and comfortable with the role I was playing in our human's life. We heard him say one day...**"It's ok for me to go. My job as loving, spiritual companion is over."** Mom and I looked at each other with alarm and a watchful eye was placed over him.

A couple of month's later. Taii passed a blood clot, paralyzing his back legs. The vet said his chances of survival would be less than 45% with tests and procedures being extremely painful. Mom sat with Taii thinking and talking it over with him. He asked to be **"let go".** His wishes were complied with. He left peacefully with his paw on top of mom's hand. We grieved and mourned together. This ritual is very important to us as well. Don't leave us out. We need assurance and love at that time as well.

For years after Taii's death, whenever a pure white tom was seen, I would get excited saying **"look, look it's Taii."** I would be gently reminded that it was another cat lucky enough to look like him and that he was on the other side watching over us.

I know my time is near. I am not ready to leave my human that I love with my heart and soul, but my body is starting to shut down.

Illness

You will be grateful for developing your intuition and spiritual nature and telepathic skills. You will consider it a blessing when having to comfort us through our illnesses. It helps you to be productive instead of helpless. It can at times save our lives. Don't forget the heart-to-heart connection.

My human kept the heart-to-heart connection with me constantly. This helped make my last years with her a beautiful, spiritual journey for both of us. As my time grew closer, I would sleep in her arms while she rocked me. Our hearts and souls were connected. We spoke heart-to-heart, telepathically. These became our moments of complete peace.

There are different methods of determining your pet's level of pain and books written on it. Check the Resource Section in the back of the book.

My mom's favorite method was the pendulum. She learned to use it as a pain meter and to determine the amount of nutrition or medication to give me. She would simply hold the pendulum in one hand and gently place her other hand on my body. At times when I was agitated and didn't want to be touched, she would hold her hand near without touching me and ask the question of where I was hurting. When that was determined, she would have the pendulum go side to side for "no" back and forth for "yes" and start counting from 1-10 to determine the pain threshold I was in. The pendulum would stop moving at a number helping to determine whether we were in a crises or not and how to proceed.

This can also be done where the pendulum moves clockwise to your count for pain intensity. A bit of practice with the pendulum is an excellent source of information for the both of you and if a vet is needed. Record all observations to bring to the vet. The more details provided, the better.

A pendulum is simply a small crystal (they can be purchased at many book or specialty stores) or ring attached on a string, chain or piece of yarn about 10-12" long. Hold it in one hand while placing your other hand gently and lightly on the animal or close to him if he is agitated for some reason. It helps to get into a meditative state and breathe slowly and calmly before doing this. It will inadvertently calm your animal and you to get the clear pictures needed for proper diagnosis and images coming from your pet.

Please talk to your pet before transporting him to the vet, or anywhere else for that matter. Humans can be so dense where we are concerned. Communicate with us. Lower our stress level by explaining what will happen to us and why. When you are coming back for us. Talk to us in front of the vet. Ask the vet to cooperate as well. Don't lie. Be honest. This will help prepare us. This also makes a difference in our being a cooperative patient.

My vets always called me a sweet, wonderful, cooperative patient. Even in times of crises, I could hear my human talk to me telepathically. Everyone can achieve this level of communication. Practice makes success!

Be upfront with what you are sensing after talking to us verbally and telepathically or working the pendulum. Don't care what others think. This is between you and your animal. It has been proven too many times that your feelings on your animal, conveyed to the vet, are correct and can make the difference in a faster, accurate diagnosis. You live with your animal and you know him best. Vets are happy to listen and receive information. If your vet doesn't take time to listen to you and talk to your pet, then it's time to change doctors for the best interest of your animal and your peace of mind.

Talk to your animal to see if prescribed medicine and treatments are working. **We know our own bodies. Please listen to us**. Sometimes a second opinion is necessary. Involve us in our treatments. We recover more quickly when being treated as part of the process, not kept in the dark. **We do hear your thoughts. Never forget that!**

Carol Gurney has some wonderful healing techniques and goes into wonderful detail in her book "7 Steps to Communicating with Animals", regarding Alternative Medicine, Body work and Energy, TellingtonTTouch, acupuncture and chiropractic treatments and homeopathy.

Quit wishing "animals could talk".
We can and we do.
Develop your intuitive, telepathic skills
and you will open up
a whole new world for you and for us.
Love us as we love you.

We are there for you in your time
of discomfort and illness and pain.
Take time to learn to help walk us through ours.

7

Healing

There is no psychiatrist in the world
like a puppy licking your face.
Ben Williams

The native tongue with animals is intuition and telepathy. Intuitive touch and massaging methods work best and again, acknowledge the animal to be able to open up the area where energy needs to be manipulated. They will learn to look forward to your gentle touch.

Be open to all methods of healing and use other healers when needed. Pay attention to telepathic thought and energy from the animal. That will tell you if they are responding favorably to your continuing or becoming edgy or restless telling you to stop. Talk to them acknowledging you received their message.

Touch Healing

Massage—use sparingly and only short treatments 3-15 minutes, very gently, then stop. You may have to repeat another time. Let the body rest and heal.

Your animal may shy away when a sore spot is touched. Please advise and ask permission to touch him. Touch gently and firmly. Start on the head and neck first. talk to him gently. Tell him what you're doing. If he jumps when touched at a certain spot, let off for a moment. Then continue, slowly, gently. When relief is accomplished, your animal will relax. Talk to him, let him know you are finished.

If your animal protests, stop and continue later. Always talk to him. A little bit of touch is better than nothing. Calmness, firmness and gentleness is important. Anyone can do it. Keep in contact with him while working on him. Keep positive thoughts with a loving environment. Stop confused ill at ease thinking with him.

Laying on of Hands

Laying on of Hands, projects positive energy into the animal. You can move hands all over the body. Rinse your hands after healing to not absorb their energy. Reiki healing is fantastic. Acknowledge and release any negative feelings picked up when tending to your animal. You can develop intuitive touch and your animal will tell you where to lay hands on. For in depth healing, refer to Penelope Smith's Healing and Counseling with Animals books and tapes) or Carole Gurney—The language of Animals 7 Steps to Communicating with Animals book)

8

Sam's Last Days

We are not here to stay. We are here to go.
Dr. Werner vonBraun

Wednesday, Nov 6, 2002

It is obvious that Sam is approaching the light more and more. I am sitting on the porch swing, gently rocking and holding her in my arms. She has her face into the wind, breathing the teasing touches of cooler weather. We are immersed in complete peace and calmness.

My upstairs friend and neighbor Sue Ann is walking her dog Chompers and stops to visit. Chompers is his usual excited self, jumping on the gate, wanting to reach Sam to say Hi. Sam leans her head over the gate and Chompers suddenly becomes quiet and sits down. He knows that he is in the presence of his friend looking into the light. They have a conversation between the two of them for a few minutes.

Sue Ann instinctually knows what Sam needs. She gently pets her head and keeps telling her that it is all right to leave the earth. Telling her what a wonderful dog she is, Sam is told of the people and other animals that will be on the other side to greet her. She impresses on her the fact that she doesn't have to take care of her mom any longer, that she has loving friends that will take care of her and not to worry about her.

God Bless her. Sam is hearing from someone else that I will be all right and that there are people around me that love me. Sam looks very hard at her as she is saying this. She then looks at me very carefully, deep into my heart, which I open up completely for her to see and feel, to determine if I am lying and asks me if this is true. I reassure her through my tears that, yes, it is true and for her to relax and not worry about me. Her responsibility is over and that it is now time for her to continue her journey into the light. I can feel her attitude and demeanor change. There is final acceptance and from that moment on, we both make sure to share every moment possible to talk quietly, lovingly, sharing thoughts and words like loving friends and companions do.

I thank Sue Ann for those words to Sam. It sometimes takes someone not as close to your pet for words to take meaning. I know when Sam hears those words from me, she thinks that I am just trying to make her feel better, and will not let herself believe.

The difference in her heart is palpable. Yes, she is clingy. That is the way it is when two souls with such a heart-to-heart connection are getting ready to part. Except for the normal reaction of being distressed when trying to breathe, I can feel the calmness that has entered her heart and soul. I can feel her finally releasing her responsibility to me. I can finally feel her accepting my unconditional love.

Sam's Last Picture
June 2002

She is finally allowing herself to receive my sense of responsibility to her in her last days. I take her to a new vet and get medication to help make her comfortable. We recognize that we are coming to the end of her life cycle.

Thursday, Nov 7, 2002

Sam comes into my bedroom around 430am and seems uncomfortable. I can hear her snuffing through her nose. I can hear her calling to me. I picked her up, took her to our rocker and can tell she is struggling for breath. I hold her upright laying her on my chest and little by little, the breathing calms down to a point where I think she has stopped breathing completely. I can feel her slipping away. Something happens to distract that peace and she is back with the living once again. She manages to eat a couple of chicken sticks. She's not interested in the rest of her breakfast, which she would devour on other days.

She follows me around, not wanting me out of her sight, then will stand and wait for me to pick her up and hold her close to me again. It is my prayer that she goes peacefully in her sleep or when I am holding her. I know she is moving toward the light. Yes, I will cry with sadness, but also with happiness for her to finally be free from pain. Other than being tired, I am peaceful and keep reassuring and encouraging her that everything is more than all right and she can leave when she is ready. She is almost there, but still needs my assurance and is enjoying the body contact where our hearts are physically close.

I know I have Sam longer than meant, wonderful bonus years and time. Dr. Betsy Coville, a wonderful alternative, homeopathic doctor helped to extend an additional three years together. I truly believe in alternative, homeopathic doctors and would love to see a marriage between conventional and alternative, homeopathic medicine. I believe with all my heart that there are times when both are needed.

March of 2002, while in meditation, I am told that Sam will be with me until September or October. I receive 11 bonus days with her in November. The universe pushes her to the point that I have to make the decision to help her in spite of herself. It is the hardest decision I ever had to m make. Her pain becomes so intense and excruciating and the choice is taken out of my hands. There is no decision but to help her make that final journey to freedom.

Friday, November 8, 2002

Everything remains the same. The medicine dulls the pain and she is only interested in her favorite snacks and liverwurst. It is my pleasure to accommodate her tastes.

Saturday, November 9, 2002

The medication helps her sleep hours and hours. When awake, she dozes in my arms and nibbles on her snacks. She has become the ultimate infant.

Sunday, November 10, 2002

She has stopped going outdoors. It is too difficult to do much walking. Thank God for piddle pads. She is changing once again. Her spirit seems more distant, but still wants to be held for short periods of time. I think for my comfort rather than hers.

Monday, November 11, 2002

A follow-up visit to the vet brings the conversation to euthanasia and the need to think strongly on it. I set up the time for tomorrow to help her cross over. Blood work is done to determine how the kidneys are functioning. Results are due back in a few hours. What happened next, makes me wonder if I missed Samantha's signal and her saying "goodbye" to me.

When the vet comes to take her for her blood work, Sam looks at me deeply. I misunderstand her. I reassure her that she is coming home with me. I realize with the later events that day, that she was in reality saying **"Goodbye".** I truly believe her spirit of awareness left at that moment. What goes home with me is a shell of a body that needs release.

Returning home, she becomes very agitated and keeps going in and out onto the patio. I realize that she is constantly straining and realize that she is going into kidney failure. A call to the vet and the blood work confirms my fear that her kidneys are shutting down. I hurry to the vet and pick up different pain medication that was easier to administer. This seems to help and Sam goes to sleep. She wakes up after 7pm when the vet is closed and it is too late for me to take her there for them to administer euthanasia.

It doesn't matter what I try to do, the pain escalates to extreme measures. Sue Ann drives us to the emergency room. Sam is in such distress that she starts to bark. Something she hasn't done for almost two years, with her hearing loss. It is now up to me to be her friend and release her from this earth plane, out of pain and suffering, to help her make the journey to freedom. She is bound and determined to stay by me regardless of how she is suffering. The time has come.

I cannot say enough good things about the Florida Veterinary Specialists, Dr. Berlin, technicians and staff. They are sincere, caring humans that understand the emotions of the human involved in this kind of situation. With their help, Samantha is released from pain around 830pm.

After the first shot of barbiturate, her body slumps with such relief, making it easy to feel the release of her spirit soaring into the tunnel and the events that lead her quickly into the City of Lights. After the second shot to stop her heart, I hold her in my arms, crying with sadness at her leaving me and happiness that she is free from pain. I know she is grateful to be free from pain and from this poor body that disintegrated.

Death is but a passage out of a prison into a palace.
Dr. Werner vonBraun

Death

Let us pass on with dignity, respect and love.

We have a shorter lifespan than humans. We live in today. We are in tune with nature and the rhythm of life and death. In spite of this, we do not leave until we feel our job is done.

I have kept myself alive longer than my contracted life-span for a couple of reasons. I love my human with all my heart and soul and I need to know she will be safe and secure without me. Her love and attendance to my ills continues to give strength to my body. My spirit is strong and sustaining, but not for much longer. The pain is increasing. My human already knows my date of departure. I cannot stay longer. She is learning acceptance of the time left.

Consult with us. Ask if we are ready to leave.

I frighten mom when my back legs suddenly start to kick out to the back and sides, seeming to have a life of their own. I then proceed to have spells where my body trembles as if very cold. I am picked up, held close to her body, wrapped in a blanket. Her hands gently massage me while she coos softly into my heart.. **"There, there, little one, you're okay, you're ok.. I love you."**

My body stops trembling and I feel fine enough to get down from her arms and act like nothing has happened. I hear her ask, **"Are you ready to leave? I will be safe without you. Please release your responsibility of taking care of me. It is ok for you to go. I love you."**

In order to make sure she is really receiving a clear message from me saying **"Not yet."** She asks a couple of her friends that are very intuitive to ask me as well. On hearing their discussion, I come out from my resting place saying very loudly…**"I'm, not ready to go. Please stop asking and talking about it."** My wishes are complied with and not another word is said until close to the last day of departure on November 11, 2002.

It is important to see if physical ailments are treatable. We can have jerking limbs, ministrokes, chronic diseases and still have life left to live. Don't be too hasty to pull the plug on us. Also, don't be selfish and keep us around when a vet is suggesting that since our quality of life is gone, it is time to think of our well being and letting us go. Talk to us. Ask us at that point if we are ready and if we have any last requests.

I am prepared for my leaving and have finally come to grips with it. Many of our conversations in the last month consist of talking about the great, wonderful and sometimes crazy adventures we shared. Loving praise on what a wonderful companion, guardian and friend I was. How I was always appreciated for my intelligence, humor and love. How I will be missed and how I will be loved forever in her heart. How we will be together again in spirit one day or in another incarnation.

It doesn't matter if you know the date that we will depart or not. Death hits with a deafening blow. Leaving an empty hole in the heart and spirit. Even knowing that spirit is energy and ongoing, the physical void is what is difficult to handle at first and can be ongoing for some time. When it is our time to go, it is our time. It will not matter what treatments or medications are used.

When November 11th comes. The date to help me cross over is set for the next morning on November 12th. Not to be. I refuse all medications, turn away from food and water on the 11th. The pain that had been held in check comes surging forward breaking through all of my reserves to hold it back. My body is shutting down. My kidneys are failing.

I cry with the terrible pain. My human, my loving mom wraps me in a blanket and with the help of Sue Ann, takes me to the emergency room. I no longer want to be on earth. I want help to release me from the body that has failed me.

After they prep me with an iv catheter, my mom holds me in her arms. The doctor injects the barbiturate into my vein. **SUDDEN FREEDOM! NO PAIN!** I am soaring away from earth with tremendous speed into loving, gentle hands. There is the sound of wings around me. There is love. There is peace. There is no mom. I look back. The shot to stop my heart hasn't been administered yet. I can still return.

Gentle hands, and loving voices stop me. I hear my mom say to the doctor. **"Samantha's spirit is free. She is gone. Please finish and stop the heart. It is over."**

Thank you my loving human.
my loving friend.
Thank you for giving me freedom.

My wish is for everyone on earth to experience this kind of bond and understanding with each other and with all species. It takes time, patience and love to perfect. It is attainable.

Honor us and the life you share with us.
Learn to love us enough to let us go
when the time is here.
That is the greatest act of love,
bravery and friendship we can ask of you.
Preserve our dignity.
Death leaves a heartache no one can heal.
Love leaves a message no one can steal.
From a headstone in Ireland

Grief

Don't be shocked that you feel grief at our passing. Who else loves you so unconditionally? Who else teaches you to love yourself the way we love you? Let yourself grieve. Help yourself through it. Get with a support group. Your vet or the internet can help you connect with one.

We are happy in the afterlife. Please complete the cycle of grieving before bringing in another animal to fill the void. You will not be giving the newcomer a fair chance. There will be comparisons to your deceased pet. Your mixed emotions will confuse the newcomer.

Also give the new animal a different name. Avoid using the name of the deceased. Each of us is unique in a special way. Bringing in our own special talents, quirks and personalities. Each of has a different job.

The pain passes, but the beauty remains.
Pierre Auguste Penoir…

Dealing with My Personal Grief

My grief is intense. I am bereft. My loving, beautiful creature known as Samantha is gone. I am able to come to terms and rationalize that she is out of pain. I know that life is energy and doesn't end. The spirit goes on. I miss the physical comfort I received and gave to her in return. Ministering to her daily needs, helping her eat, became a form of meditation and a very spiritual experience.

I am not in a hurry for the universe to speed things up to a time when the grief will be easier to handle and less pain. The pain and loss when we love so deeply is part of that portion of life. Bittersweet. That is the basis of wonderful, successful love of any kind.

Even though I was in touch with nature in every aspect before. I didn't realize the full aspect of communicating with other species and that I was doing it, until Sam came into my life. I was under the false impression, that everyone talked to animals. It was second nature to me, like talking to my child or another human.

To the outside world Samantha was my "little politician". In reality, she was my teacher. She was there when I was going through a difficult time with my health. We communicated from the first day she came into my life.

We were already communicating when I was on my way to pick her up from my son's house. She informed me that her name was to be **"Samantha".** A very feminine, southern name. She became known to everyone that had the honor to be in her life somehow as **"Sam".** Her personal job to me was to make me aware of the lack of understanding between most humans and their animals. This bridge of understanding had to be built. I know she left earth to free me from tending to her ailments. Free me to teach others this wonderful gift of communication.

I temporarily pull away from talking to people. I spend time reading articles written on grief, guilt, euthanasia, the pros and cons to natural death, fear that Sam was put down too soon. I read everything I can find. This helps me open up to cry my pain and unhappiness at the universe. I have to writhe and finish feeling the pain that Sam was in that last evening. I have to feel the deliverance of her spirit completely when given that blessed barbiturate shot that put her into that deep sleep of release. I have to feel her spirit once again flying out of that pain riddled body. I have to feel her come to a complete stop. I have to feel her freedom, her joy of spirit life. And I have to forgive myself for thinking I didn't do enough to help her. After experiencing every moment of November 11th, I am able to wake up one morning feeling cleansed and lighter in spirit. I am able to feel her unconditional love once again.

9

From One Heart to Another in Spirit

After Death Communication

Through creature and creation
One can reach or realize divinity
St. Francis Assisi

Returning from the emergency room on the 11th, I fall into an exhausted sleep around 5am and have a dream that shows me what takes place immediately after Sam's death.

I am looking through emergency room windows (similar but different from the one we are in on the 11th) and see doctors and angels around her. They are holding Sam in an upright position brushing her body with their hands and wings, making all illness and years melt away. Every time they make a sweeping motion over her, she becomes younger and healthier. She looks vibrant and is looking right at me with her wonderful, bright eyes and smiling.

I am so happy seeing her like that. Without feeling any urgency to be with her. We gaze at each other with peace and love. I understand that she is going through a wonderful, rapid metamorphosis and that she is more than all right. She is healing rapidly and being prepared to enter the City of Lights.

You can still communicate with us after we're gone from life. Sound crazy? Why? Love doesn't end after death. We come to you in your dreams. We visit you at home. You may hear us sneeze or do something easily recognized. We send other creatures as messengers to help you through your grieving. If you have learned your lessons well and practiced your communication and telepathic skills with us when we were alive, you will be able to connect with us after we are gone.

Follow the rules of communication talked about in earlier chapters. Then do the following—become quiet, breathe deeply, meditate, release tension from your mind and body, open your heart core, reach out. Wait and see. If nothing happens at first don't give up. Sometimes we are busy. Patience! Try later on the next day. You will receive thoughts and images, as before. Talk to us. Share your feelings. Ask questions. Trust the connection you had in the past.

I have been in communication with my human many times since I have left. I have gently licked off her tears from her grief. I have snuffled in her ear, telling her I love her. I have come to her in her dreams, giving her the privilege of seeing me in my healing process. I have come to her through Chompers, Sue Ann's dog. I kiss her through him.

The day after I passed on, with Chompers' permission, I came into his body and ran into the house, laughing and hollering at mom in my mind, **"See me. See how healthy I am. See how energetic and wonderful I am again. I thank you.. I love you."** Mom laughed and cried with happiness.

Sati, who is normally afraid and unfriendly toward other dogs and cats, just stood there in amazement and wondered why I looked different. **I am alive. I am well. I am young. I continue on…**

December 11th one month after my passing on, mom goes into deep meditation after writing the closing chapters of this book and crying over the memories stirred by those last words.

Communicating with us after death sometimes takes time because we can be busy. That is the situation for mom today. She sits quietly, in peace, waiting to see if I am available. I'm not and am not able to just pop in at that moment. My wonderful human just continues to sit there in peace, sending her unconditional love to me.

Mom being who she is, however, has certain privileges over here and I am given permission to let her see what I am involved in. I am not just chasing squirrels, although I do enjoy that. I ran myself silly after those crazy creatures for the first two days I was here. Having not barked for the past year and a half until the day I was dying, I lost my voice from barking so much out of happiness and joy when I first arrived.

Oh well, I am digressing. Sorry. Mom is given permission to see what my present job is. I am still **"the little politician"** and also **"official greeter".** I help souls coming through the tunnel to the City of Lights. Along with the light they see at the end of the tunnel, they hear my barking and it helps guide them. It gives them happiness to realize that their animals are there for them when they arrive. I was proud to let mom see me working at the entrance to the City of Lights.

December 11th, 2002—**One Month Anniversary of my death. My human and myself, we visit in spirit. She celebrates not my death, but my rebirth. I can feel her pride and love. I send her mine.**

Bibliography and Resources

Animal Communication and Spiritual

Goodall, Jane, with Berman, Phillip. *Reason for Hope: A Spiritual Journey.* New York: Warner Books, 1999

Gurney, Carol. *The Language of Animals: 7 Steps to Communicating with Animals.* Random House, Inc. 2001

Hauser, Marc D. *Wild Animals: What Animals Really Think.*
Henry Holt and Company, LLC, 2000

Masson, Jeffrey Moussaeieff, and McCarthy, Susan. *When Elephants Weep: The Emotional Lives of Animals.* New York:
Delacorte Press, 1995

Page, George. *Inside the Animal Mind: A Groundbreaking Exploration of Animal Intelligence.* Doubleday 1999

Smith, Penelope. *Animal Talk, Interspecies Telepathic Communication, Second Edition.* Hillsboro, OR: Beyond Words Publishing, Inc. 1999

Smith, Penelope, *Interspecies Telepathic Connection Tape Series* (six one-hour audiotapes). Available from Upper Access at (800) 356-9315 or on the web at upperaccess.com

Weaver, Helen. *The Daisy Sutra: Conversations with My Dog.* Buddha Rock Press 2001

Death and Dying

Eadie, Betty J. *Embraced by the Light.* New York:
Bantam Books, 1994]

Montgomery, Mary and Herb. *A Final Act of Caring: Ending the Life of an Animal Friend.* Minneapolis: Montgomery Press, 1992

Weiss, Brian L. *Many Lives, Many Masters.* New York: Simon and Schuster, 1988

Alternative Health Care

McKay, Pat. *Reigning Cats and Dogs: Good Nutrition, Healthy Happy Animals.* South Pasadena, CA: Oscar Publications 1992.

Pitcairn, Richard H. D.V.M., and Pitcairn, Susan Hubble. *Dr. Pitcairn's Complete Guide to Natural Health for Dogs & Cats.* Emmaus, PA: Rodale Pres, 1995

Tellington-Jones, Linda, with Taylor, Sybil. *The Tellington TTouch. A Breakthrough Technique to Train and Care for your Favorite Animal.* New York, Viking Press, 1992.

Animal's Understanding of Time

Sheldrake, Rupert, *Dogs That Know When Their Owners Are Coming Home and Other Unexplained Powers of Animals: An Investigation.* New York Crown Publishing, 1999

Alternative Health Care
Betsy Colville, D.V.M.
Alternative Animal Care
813-949-1818

Healing—Body, Mind and Spirit
Northdale's Family Chiropractic
Bruce D. Horchak. D.C.
Chiropractic Physician
14855 N. Dale Mabry Hwy
Tampa, Florida, 33618
813-960-8447

Lost and Found
Animal Recovery
www.pmia.com
offers free listings.

National Pet Recovery
800-934-8638
www.petrecovery.com

Pet Finder
800-274-2556
www.petfindersalert.com

90 Samantha's Love Story

Miscellaneous
Joseph Witowsky
website designer
jawitowsky@tanjintdesign.com
www.Tanjintdesign.com

About the Author

Ms. Patricia Daniels, comes from Russian/Polish ancestry. She has helped hundreds of people with her gifts of dream interpretation, counseling and life coaching for over 38 years. World-renown with her accurate visions, it wasn't long before she realized that her blessings were not only for the communication with people, but animals as well. It quickly became apparent that she was understanding and hearing their thoughts and words.

Ms. Daniels teaches adults and children how to communicate and make a spiritual connection with animals through lectures and workshops. Patricia teaches at Baywinds Learning Centre and privately. She presently resides in Tampa, Florida. Her love of animals, has brought her to a life goal of bringing awareness to the value of animals' intellect and loving natures.

Visit her at her website.

www.talktoyouranimal.com
talktoyouranimal@yahoo.com
pat@talktoyouranimal.com

To help protect the animal population,
have your pets spayed or neutered.
Bob Barker

0-595-31065-6